The Little Mermaid

Retold by Enid C. King
with illustrations by Victoria Assanelli

LADYBIRD TALES

FAR AWAY IN THE DEEP,
deep sea stood the Mer-king's
palace. He lived there with
six lovely daughters and their
grandmother. The youngest
daughter had sea-blue eyes and
delicate skin. Like all mermaids,
she had no legs. Instead she had
a tail like a fish.

The mermaid princesses
collected things that had fallen
from passing ships to decorate
their gardens.

The youngest princess chose
just to grow red flowers and a
single red tree. In the middle
of her garden was a statue of a
young boy.

Most of all the youngest princess enjoyed hearing about the world above the sea. She would ask her grandmother again and again to tell her about flowers you could smell and creatures called birds that flew through the trees.

"When you are fifteen, you can rise to the surface of the sea and see all these things for yourself," said her grandmother.

It would be a year before her oldest sister became fifteen. Each sister was a year younger than the last, so it would be six whole years before the youngest would see the world. The oldest sister promised to tell them all she had seen when her turn came.

Sometimes at night the youngest princess would look up through the clear blue water. She could see the pale glow of the stars and the moon. Sometimes a large shadow passed overhead and she knew this must be either a whale or a ship. She liked to imagine it was a ship, full of the strange beings who lived above the waves. She wished she could see them for herself.

At last the day came when the oldest princess could rise to the surface of the sea. All her sisters waited eagerly for her to come back. Then they listened while she told them of a town near the coast.

"There were hundreds of lights," she said, "and music and the sound of bells from tall church towers."

The youngest princess was even more impatient. The next year the second daughter had her turn. She came back and talked about a vivid sunset, with clouds of gold and red and violet. She had seen a flock of birds fly overhead and described how beautiful they looked. The youngest daughter wished so hard for her turn to come.

When the third princess became fifteen she was very brave and swam up a great river. She had seen the hills and the trees and the houses and castles. She told of the sun that was hot on her face and the children that swam in the water, although they had no tails.

The fourth sister did not go so far. She spoke of the ships sailing by and the whales spouting water. Her sister, the fifth princess, saw many different things.

It was winter when she rose to the surface. She talked about icebergs and storms and huge black clouds. She told of great flashes of lightning and rolls of thunder.

After a time, the five sisters preferred to stay at home. Sometimes, however, they all rose to the surface. Hand in hand, they sang sweetly to the sailors on the ships, who thought it was the wind. The youngest mermaid sat in her father's palace and wished even harder for her turn to come.

At long last, the great day came. The little mermaid rose up until her head was above the surface.

The sun had just set. There was no wind and the sea was smooth. A large ship lay still on the water, and the little mermaid could hear music and singing coming from it.

A wave lifted her so she could see into the cabin. It was the prince's birthday and all the men on board were enjoying a party. The prince was a handsome young man. When he came on deck they set off hundreds of fireworks and the little mermaid was frightened. She hid underwater, but soon came back to the surface. She wanted to see the handsome prince again.

While she waited and watched, a storm blew up. The wind howled and the ship was tossed about like a toy boat. Suddenly a great gust of wind turned it over. The water rushed in and broke it in pieces. The little mermaid searched for the prince in the darkness. She was afraid he had drowned when the ship sank. She knew that humans could not live under water as she could.

A flash of lightning showed her where the prince was. He was almost drowned and he was too tired to swim any more. She took hold of him and kept his head above the waves.

When morning came the prince still had his eyes closed. The little mermaid took the prince to a bay with smooth dry sand and laid him in the warm sun. There was a building nearby with bells ringing from it. The little mermaid swam out to sea and waited.

Some of the people from the building came out and found the prince. They were worried because they thought he was dead. Soon, the prince got better and the people were glad. They took him into a house and the little mermaid was sad. The prince would never know who had saved him. She dived below the waves and went to her father's palace.

Her sisters asked her what she had seen. She only told them about a ship and a house and said no more. She often went back to the bay hoping to see the prince, but he was never there.

She felt so sad that, at last, she told one of her sisters the whole story. One of them knew who the handsome prince was and where he lived.

Together, all the princesses swam up to his palace. Now that the little mermaid knew where the prince lived, she went there often. She was very brave and swam close to the land to watch the prince. She was happy to think that she had saved him.

The little mermaid wished she were a human being, and she went to talk to her grandmother.

"Do men live for ever if they do not drown?" asked the princess.

"No, they die, just as we die. But their life is much shorter than ours. We live to be three hundred years old. But when we die we just become foam on the sea. Humans have souls," said her grandmother.

"I think I would rather be a human, just for one day," said the little mermaid. "I would happily give up my three hundred years if I could have a soul, like the humans."

"You can only get a soul if a human loves you," said her grandmother. "But that won't happen because they do not like our tails."

This made the little princess sad. "I must do something," she said to herself. And, while her sisters were busy dancing at the court ball, she went to see the witch.

The witch's house was in a wood beside the bog. It was made of bones, and the witch sat inside stroking a large toad.

"I know what you have come for," the witch said. "You want legs like the humans, instead of your beautiful tail, so that the prince may love you. You are foolish, but you can have your wish."

The witch laughed. "I will tell you what you must do. You must take a magic drink and swim to the surface. Sit on the rocks and drink it. Your tail will split in two and turn into legs. It will be very painful. If you think you can stand the pain I will help you."

"Oh yes, I'm sure I can," said the little mermaid, thinking of the handsome prince.

"Remember," said the witch, "once you turn into a human you can never turn back again. If the prince doesn't marry you, you will never get a human soul. The day he marries someone else you will die. You will become foam on the sea, like other mermaids."

"I still want to try it," said the little mermaid.

In return for the magic drink, the witch demanded the best thing the little mermaid owned – her voice.

"But if I have no voice, how will I win the prince?"

"You will have to use your grace and charm and your beautiful eyes," said the witch.

Sadly, the little mermaid agreed. The witch set up her cauldron and it boiled and bubbled.

"Here it is," said the witch handing her a bottle. The little mermaid became dumb, and she swam back home with the drink.

When the princess came to her father's palace, everyone was asleep. She wanted to go and say goodbye but she couldn't speak.

She picked a flower from each of her sisters' gardens to remind her of home, then she swam to where the prince lived.

She sat in the dark on the marble staircase and drank the magic liquid. She felt a sharp pain and then she fainted.

She woke in the morning to see that her tail had become two slim legs. Before her was the handsome prince. He asked who she was and how she got there, but she could only smile at him.

The prince led the little mermaid into the palace and found her some beautiful clothes to wear. Everyone said how gracefully she walked, but the little mermaid was sad because she couldn't talk.

When a young servant girl sang it made her even sadder. She knew she used to have a voice far sweeter than that.

But when the servant girls danced, she joined in. She was so light and graceful, everyone stopped to watch her. The prince, especially, was enchanted. He said she must always stay with him. She slept in a nearby room, and went with him everywhere. But all the time her feet hurt her, as the witch had told her they would.

At night time, the little mermaid went down the steps of the palace to bathe her feet in the sea.

One evening, her sisters came to see her. The next evening they brought her grandmother with them and her father, too.

The prince grew very fond of the little mermaid, but he did not ask her to be his wife.

One day he said to her.

"You remind me of a girl I saw once. My ship was wrecked in a storm, and when I woke up, a girl had helped me to shore. She saved my life. I shall never forget her, but she is the only person I could love."

The little mermaid could not tell the prince the truth because she had given away her voice.

One day, she heard that he was going on a journey to see a princess in another country.

"My parents hope I will marry her," said the prince. "But if I can't marry the girl who saved me, I would rather marry you."

He and the little mermaid travelled by ship, and each night her sisters swam up to see her.

The next day, they reached the city. There was a procession in the street. When the princess arrived she was very beautiful.

When the prince saw her he was amazed. "You are the girl who saved my life," he said. He turned to the little mermaid and said, "I did not dare to hope that I would see this girl again. You must be happy too, for you have always loved me more than anyone else."

The little mermaid thought her heart would break. She knew that the day the prince got married, she would die.

At the wedding, she walked behind the princess and carried her train. That night, they all went on board the ship. There was a special tent in the middle of the deck for the prince and princess. It had soft beds and lovely silk curtains.

After the party, when everyone had gone to bed, the little mermaid watched the sun rise, knowing that she would die.

Suddenly her sisters appeared. "We gave our hair to the witch to use for magic," they said. "She has given us this sharp knife. If you use it to kill the prince, you will become a mermaid again. Hurry, before the sun rises."

The little mermaid took the knife, but she could not kill the prince. Instead, she threw it into the sea.

She took one last look at the prince. Then she threw herself into the sea. Slowly she turned into foam.

As the sun rose the little mermaid felt its warmth and was lifted into the sky, surrounded by strange lights and sweet voices.

"Where are you taking me?" she asked.

"To join the daughters of the air," the voices said. "Mermaids do not have souls, and neither do the daughters of the air. But we can earn our souls by the good deeds we do. If you help us, in three hundred years you may have a soul."

On the ship, the prince and princess searched for the beautiful girl who could not speak. They could not see the little mermaid, smiling at them as she drifted past behind a cloud.

A History of
The Little Mermaid

The story of *The Little Mermaid* was written by the Danish poet and author Hans Christian Andersen in 1837, and has been retold countless times in various forms since.

Originally written as a ballet, it has been adapted into various books, films and stage productions, including an animation by Disney in 1989 and a musical by Disney Theatrical in 2008.

Perhaps the most famous image of the little mermaid is the statue on a rock in Copenhagen, the capital of Denmark. Unveiled in 1913, it is one of the city's major tourist attractions.

Well-loved by generations of children, this moving tale of a young mermaid's desire to become human and gain an immortal soul continues to be popular today.

Ladybird's 1980 retelling, written by Enid C. King, captures the little mermaid's story with sensitivity and charm.

Collect more fantastic

LADYBIRD 🐞 TALES

Little Red Riding Hood

9781409311126

Goldilocks and the Three Bears

9781409311119

Cinderella

9781409311072

Jack and the Beanstalk

9781409311102

The Gingerbread Man

9781409311096

The Three Little Pigs

9781409311089

The Three Billy Goats Gruff

9781409311065

Hansel and Gretel

9781409311133

Puss in Boots

9781409311225

Rapunzel

9781409311195

Rumpelstiltskin

9781409311164

The Elves and the Shoemaker

9781409311188

Snow White and the Seven Dwarfs

9781409311171

The Enormous Turnip

9781409311218

The Magic Porridge Pot

9781409311201

Sleeping Beauty

9781409311157

The Princess
and the Frog

9780718192556

Dick
Whittington

9780718192532

The
Big Pancake

9780718192549

Beauty
and the Beast

9780718192587

The Little
Red Hen

9780718192525

The Ugly
Duckling

9780718193133

The Princess
and the Pea

9780718192570

Chicken
Licken

9780718192563

The Emperor's
New Clothes

9780723271048

The Little
Mermaid

9780723271055

Pinocchio

9780723271062

Aladdin

9780723271079

Endpapers taken from series 606d,
first published in 1964

A catalogue record for this book is available from the British Library

Published by Ladybird Books Ltd
80 Strand London WC2R 0RL
A Penguin Company

001

ISBN: 978-0-72327-105-5

Printed in China